TWELVE YEARS TWELVE ANIMALS

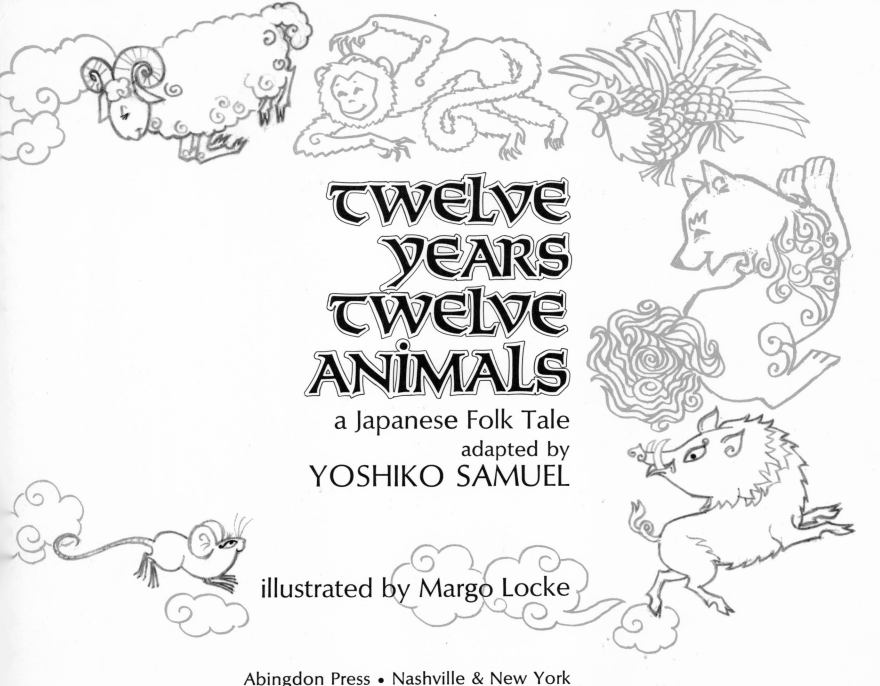

Twelve Years Twelve Animals

a Japanese Folk Tale
adapted by
YOSHIKO SAMUEL

illustrated by Margo Locke

Abingdon Press • Nashville & New York

TWELVE YEARS, TWELVE ANIMALS

Copyright © 1972 by Abingdon Press

All rights in this book are reserved.
No part of this book may be reproduced in any
manner whatsoever without written permission
of the publishers except brief quotations
embodied in critical articles or reviews. For
information address Abingdon Press, Nashville, Tennessee.
ISBN 0-687-42708-8

Library of Congress Catalog Card Number: 72-171082

Printed in the United States of America

To Mari and Sari

Long time ago
in Japan,
King decided
to invite
all the animals
to a party.
He told them
to come
to his palace
on Saturday
afternoon.

The animals were very happy to be invited, and by Friday they were all hopping and running with excitement. Tiger practiced growling so that he would be able to greet King in his best growling voice.

Dragon puffed smoke
and rattled
his scales and
said to himself,
"I am sure
King will be
pleased to see
how I do
my tricks."
Rabbit smoothed
his whiskers.

Dog cleaned his coat.
Snake was ready
for a special
snake dance, and
Ox and Sheep
practiced singing
together until
they almost lost
their voices.
They could hardly
wait for the
big party day
to come.

But poor old Cat!
He just could not
remember when
the party was
going to be given.
So he went to
his neighbor, Mouse,
and asked him,
"When are we going to
a party at King's palace?"

Mouse, who was
usually kind and
friendly, was feeling
rather mean that day.
His bad tooth was
giving him much pain.
So, without bothering
to check his calendar,
he said to Cat,
"Sunday will be the fun day."

On Saturday all the animals, but Cat,
marched together to the palace.
Mouse, with his bad tooth all taken care of,
rode on Ox's head and led the march.
After Ox came Tiger, Rabbit,
Dragon, Snake, then Horse, Sheep,
Monkey, Rooster, and finally,
Dog and Boar.
It was a noisy, happy march.

King's palace
stood tall and strong.
Its white walls
looked bright against
the clear blue sky,
and the slates
on its roofs glittered
in the spring sun
like the fish's scales.

All around
the palace ground
was a deep moat.
Swans and ducks
floated on
its blue waters.
The wind carried
the sweet scent
of cherry blossoms
from the palace yard.

Palace guards
met the animals
at the front door.
They bowed politely
to the animals
to show their
welcome and
opened the door
wide. The animals
bowed politely to
the palace guards
to show their
thanks and then
marched right into
King's party room.

King welcomed
each of his guests
with a bow.
He liked Tiger's
friendly growling
and Rabbit's
whiskers so fine
and smooth,
and thought
Dog had
the shiniest coat
he had ever seen.

Then King invited
everyone to a table
filled with food.
There were sweets
made of red beans,
crunchy rice crackers,
sugar-coated beans
in blue, green,
and gold colors,
sweet rice cakes,
sesame candy, and
fresh fruits—
peaches and pears,
oranges, grapes,
and plums.
There was sweet tea
to drink, too.

All the animals
had fun playing
games, eating fine
food, and talking
to one another. King
really enjoyed
watching Snake
dance and
listening to Ox
and Sheep sing.
And when Dragon
puffed some smoke
and rattled his
scales, King said
to himself,
"I am pleased to
know how Dragon
does his tricks."

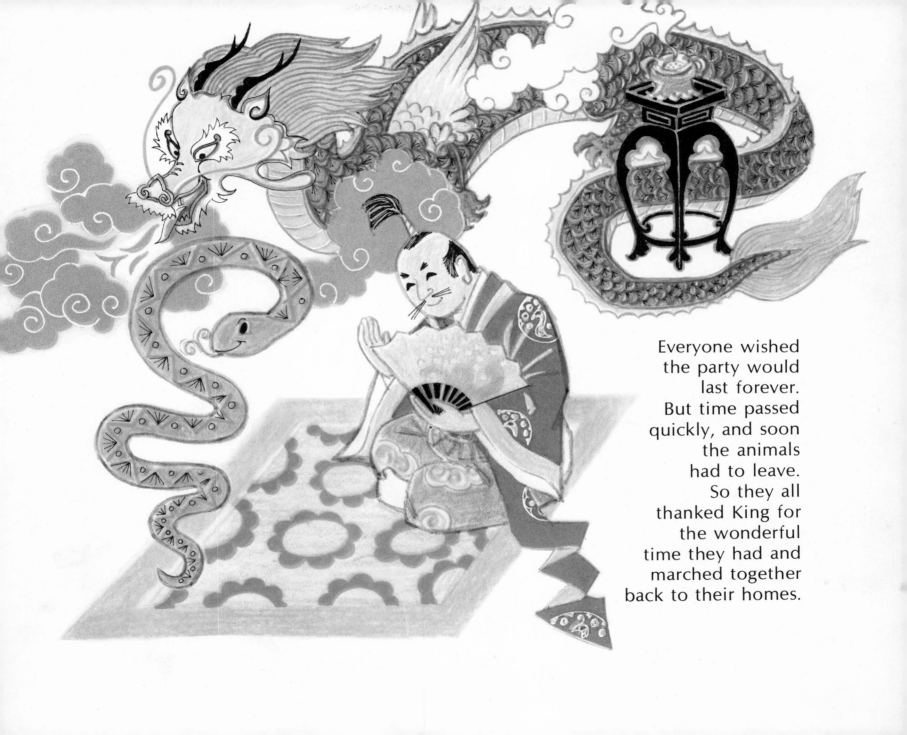

Everyone wished
the party would
last forever.
But time passed
quickly, and soon
the animals
had to leave.
So they all
thanked King for
the wonderful
time they had and
marched together
back to their homes.

King walked out onto his balcony. Watching the
early moon in the sky, its reflection on the water
in his moat, and the twelve animals marching
in between toward their homes,
he felt very happy inside.

King said to himself, "From now on I shall call each year
with the name of an animal so that I will be able to
remember all twelve of the good animal friends who came to my party.
I shall call this year the Year of the Mouse, for Mouse came first.
Next year will be the Year of the Ox, for Ox came second.
And I shall call the twelfth year from now the Year of the Boar,
for he was the last one of the animals in the march.
And then I will start again with the Year of the Mouse.

But poor Cat!

The animals' noisy homecoming
woke Cat, who could tell
they had all been to King's party.
He was angry at Mouse for
telling him the wrong day.
Later, when he learned that
each of the animals who had
been to King's party
would have a year
named for him, he
was very angry indeed.

That is why Cat and Mouse
do not get along well to this day.

Even now, Japanese people
call each year with
the name of an animal.
I was born in the Year
of the Tiger. In which
year were you born?

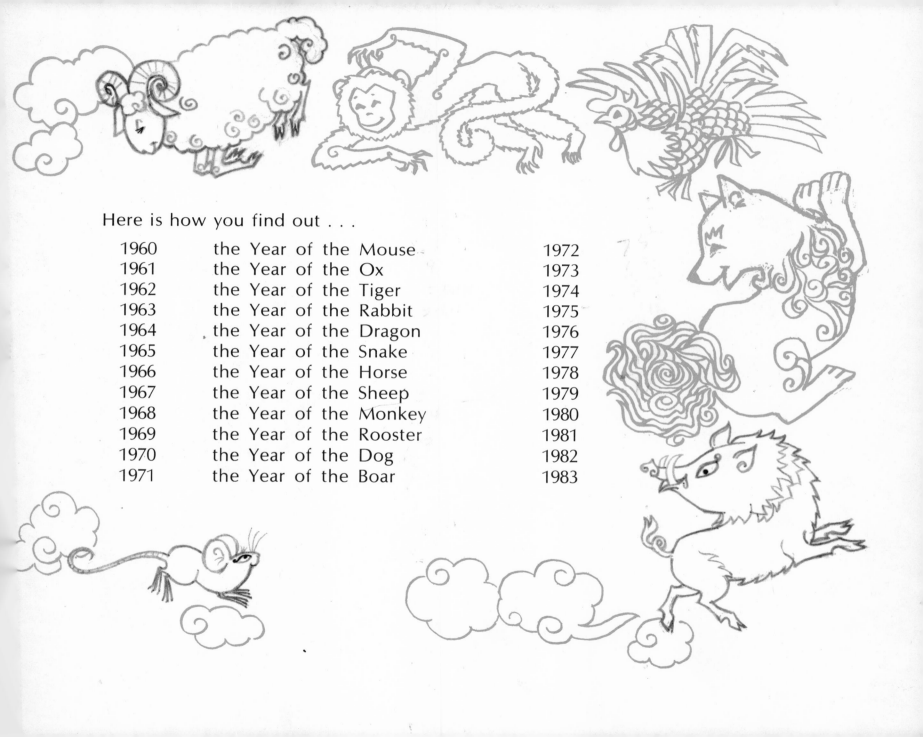

Here is how you find out . . .

1960	the Year of the Mouse	1972
1961	the Year of the Ox	1973
1962	the Year of the Tiger	1974
1963	the Year of the Rabbit	1975
1964	the Year of the Dragon	1976
1965	the Year of the Snake	1977
1966	the Year of the Horse	1978
1967	the Year of the Sheep	1979
1968	the Year of the Monkey	1980
1969	the Year of the Rooster	1981
1970	the Year of the Dog	1982
1971	the Year of the Boar	1983